DISNEY
FROZEN
Where's Olaf?

pi kids®

An imprint of Phoenix International Publications, Inc.

Chicago • London • New York • Hamburg • Mexico City • Sydney

Olaf is missing!

Olaf and his best friends are traveling all over Arendelle, from Wandering Oaken's Trading Post and Sauna to the Enchanted Forest. Can you spot them in each location?

OLAF

Sweet and innocent, Olaf is a snowman who loves warm hugs and learning about the world around him. He makes new friends wherever he travels and enjoys going on adventures with Elsa, Anna, Kristoff, and Sven.

ELSA

As a child, Elsa had to hide her magical snow powers from everyone. But now, with the support of her sister, Anna, she has overcome her fears and fully embraces these powers.

ANNA

Adventurous and kind, Anna is a caring friend. She is determined to protect her family and kingdom, no matter how dangerous a situation may be.

KRISTOFF

At times he may be a little rough around the edges, but Kristoff has a soft spot in his heart for his friends and his one true love, Anna. For a long time, Kristoff's only pal was his reindeer, Sven, and though some things have changed over the years, they are still best friends.

SVEN

Kristoff's best friend and loyal companion, Sven, is a reliable reindeer who will always help his friends when they're in trouble. Though Sven doesn't speak, Kristoff goes to him for advice when he has an important decision to make.

LOCATIONS

Look out for Olaf and his friends as they travel through the kingdom of Arendelle and beyond! In each location, you'll find Olaf, Elsa, Anna, Kristoff, and Sven as they attend a festive gathering, embark on a voyage, shop at Wandering Oaken's Trading Post and Sauna, or play in the snow. Then turn to the back of the book for even more characters and objects to find in each scene.

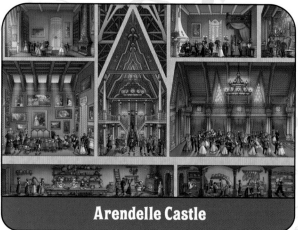

Arendelle Castle

The Great Hall

Arendelle Castle Courtyard

Ice Rink

Marketplace

Wandering Oaken's Trading Post and Sauna

Arendelle Village

Arenfjord

Valley of the Living Rock

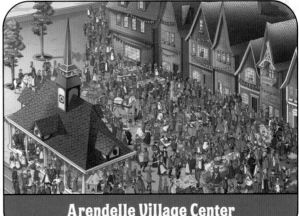

Arendelle Village Center

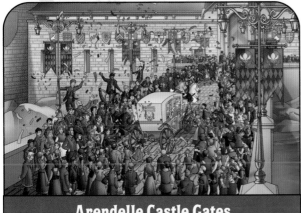

Arendelle Castle Gates

The Mountains

The Enchanted Forest

North of Arendelle

Arendelle Castle

Anna and Elsa have invited the villagers to visit their home, Arendelle Castle. While the villagers are exploring the castle, Olaf is playing hide-and-seek! Can you find where he is hiding? Where is Sven enjoying his favorite snack?

The Great Hall

Olaf and his friends are hosting a party in the Great Hall. There are couples dancing, musicians performing, and a table full of delicious desserts. What is Anna doing? Can you find Olaf among the elegant guests?

Arendelle
Castle Courtyard

The villagers have gathered in the courtyard to hear a special announcement from Elsa. Can you spot Olaf and his friends in the crowd? Who is holding the door open, welcoming guests inside?

Ice Rink

At the outdoor ice rink, some people are skating and doing tricks while others are playing in the snow. Can you spot playful Olaf among the villagers? Is Elsa skating or chatting with a friend?

Marketplace

It's a bustling day at the marketplace. The streets are filled with happy customers buying goods from friendly vendors. Can you find Olaf and his friends shopping with the villagers? Which of Olaf's friends are holding baskets?

Wandering Oaken's Trading Post and Sauna

Oaken is having his biggest blowout sale yet! Villagers from all over Arendelle have arrived to find a good bargain. As Oaken welcomes guests to his shop, can you spot Olaf in the crowd?

Arendelle Village

The villagers of Arendelle are enjoying a crisp winter evening with their neighbors and friends. Where is Olaf on this chilly night? Can you spot Anna in the crowd? Which of Olaf's friends are watching the festivities through the windows?

Arenfjord

Bon voyage! Olaf is about to depart for an adventure on the high seas. As the ships prepare for the long journey ahead, can you find Olaf, Sven, and Kristoff? Who is waving goodbye to Olaf from the shore?

Valley of the Living Rock

Olaf, Kristoff, Sven, Elsa, and Anna have just arrived at the Valley of the Living Rock. They are excited to spend time with Kristoff and Sven's troll family. Who is Olaf playing with? Can you find wise Grand Pabbie?

Arendelle Village Center

It's the Harvest Festival, and the Village Center is filled with villagers enjoying a feast, dancing, and gathering with friends. Is Olaf dancing with Anna, or is he listening to a story? Can you spot Olaf's friends enjoying the festival?

Arendelle Castle Gates

Olaf, Anna, and Elsa are arriving at Arendelle Castle after a long journey. A large crowd is gathered outside the castle gates to greet them. Where is Olaf? Can you find Sven and Kristoff among the Arendellians?

The Mountains

It's a snowy day in the mountains and the local villagers are enjoying sledding, building snowmen, and having snowball fights! How is Olaf spending his time in the wintry weather? Can you spot Elsa?

The Enchanted Forest

In the Enchanted Forest, the Arendellian soldiers and Northuldra are greeting Elsa, Anna, Olaf, Kristoff, and Sven. Is Olaf giving Sven a carrot or talking with a new friend? Where is Elsa?

North of Arendelle

Just outside of the Enchanted Forest, reindeer are playfully prancing amid the Northuldra and the Arendellian soldiers. Which spirit of nature is swirling around Olaf? Can you find Elsa, Anna, Kristoff, and Sven?

Look out for these extra characters and objects:

Arendelle Castle
- carrots
- gold trophy
- water pitcher
- vase with flowers
- painting of King Agnarr

The Great Hall
- cupcakes
- lute
- drinking glasses
- purple gloves
- fan

Arendelle Castle Courtyard
- woman holding a blue bag
- dress with a green bow
- boys talking
- blue hat
- yellow vest

Ice Rink
- snowman with sticks for hair
- scarf
- snowshoes
- sled
- snowball

Marketplace
- bread
- pumpkin
- child crawling
- baby
- scale

Wandering Oaken's Trading Post and Sauna
- troll statue
- lantern
- coat hanger
- girl holding a ball
- bottle

Arendelle Village
- chimney
- white cat
- shovel
- basket of sticks
- yellow scarf

Arenfjord
- barrel
- horse
- wooden swan
- anchor
- ship's wheel

Valley of the Living Rock
- necklace with three blue crystals
- troll made of snow
- necklace with two yellow crystals
- Grand Pabbie
- sitting troll

Arendelle Village Center
- basket of vegetables
- harp
- flute
- pot of soup
- fish sign

Arendelle Castle Gates
- bouquet of flowers
- guard
- blue hat
- horse
- wreath

The Mountains
- skier
- snowman wearing a hat
- ice skates
- sled
- carrot

The Enchanted Forest
- tree stump
- child holding a stick
- ice sculpture
- baby reindeer
- woman with freckles

North of Arendelle
- baby
- girl leaning against a tree
- Gale, the Wind Spirit
- braid
- walking stick

Answer Key

Olaf, Elsa, Anna, Kristoff, and Sven are circled in red. The other characters and objects to search for are circled in green. Sometimes there's more than one right answer for the extra objects—just one is circled, but if you search, you could find even more!

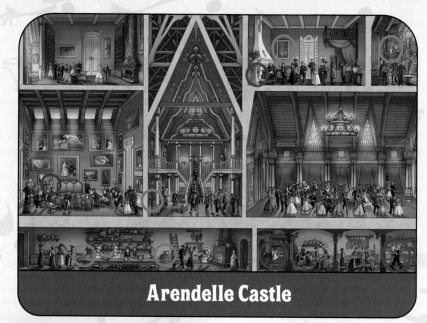
Arendelle Castle

The Great Hall

Arendelle Castle Courtyard

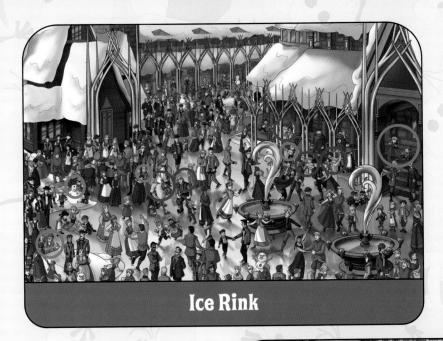

Ice Rink

Marketplace

Wandering Oaken's Trading Post and Sauna

Arendelle Village

Arenfjord

Valley of the Living Rock

Arendelle Village Center

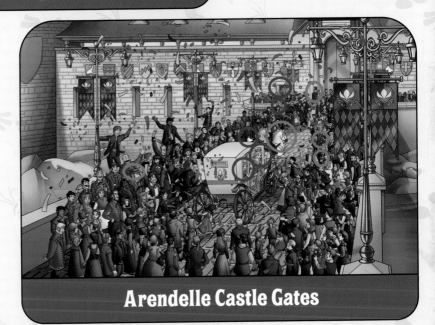

Arendelle Castle Gates

The Mountains

The Enchanted Forest

North of Arendelle